K0446

little Miss Scatterbrain

by Roger Hargreaves

First published in the United States
by Ottenheimer Publishers, Inc.

Published by Rourke Enterprises, Inc., P.O. Box 929, Windermere,
Florida 32786. Copyright © 1981 by Rourke Enterprises, Inc. All
copyrights reserved. No part of this book may be reproduced in
any form without written permission from the publisher. Printed in
the United States of America.

Library of Congress Cataloging in Publication Data

Hargreaves, Roger.
  Little Miss Scatterbrain.

  Summary: Miss Scatterbrain is forgetful indeed,
not remembering names or even where she puts her
things.
  [1. Memory—Fiction] I. Title.
PZ7.H2226.Lir 1981   [E]   81-13795
ISBN 0-86592-597-6   AACR2

ROURKE ENTERPRISES, INC.
Windermere, Florida 32786

Little Miss Scatterbrain was just a little bit forgetful.

You can say that again!

Little Miss Scatterbrain was just a little bit forgetful.

She met Mr. Funny.

"Hello, Miss Scatterbrain," he said.

"Hello, Mr. Bump," she replied.

She met Mr. Tickle.

"Hello, Miss Scatterbrain," he said.

"Hello, Mr. Strong," she replied.

She met Mr. Happy.

"Where are you off to?" he asked her.

She thought.

And thought.

"I bet you've forgotten, haven't you?" laughed Mr Happy.

Little Miss Scatterbrain looked at him.

"Forgotten what?" she said.

Miss Scatterbrain lived in the middle of the woods.

In Buttercup Cottage.

Everybody knew it was called Buttercup Cottage.

Except the owner.

She kept forgetting.

"I know," she thought to herself. "To help me remember, I'll put up a sign!"

Look what the sign says.

She isn't called little Miss Scatterbrain for nothing.

Is she?

One winter morning, she got up and went downstairs to make breakfast.

She shook some cornflakes out of the box.

But, being such a scatterbrain, she forgot to put a bowl underneath the cornflakes.

"Now, where did I put the milk?" she asked herself.

It took her ten minutes to find it.

In the oven!

After breakfast she went downtown.

Shopping.

She went into the bank first.

"Good morning, Miss Scatterbrain," smiled the bank manager.

"What can I do for you?"

Little Miss Scatterbrain looked at him.

"I'd like some . . ."

"Change?" suggested the bank manager.

"Chicken!" replied Miss Scatterbrain.

"Chicken?" exclaimed the manager. "But this isn't the butcher's. This is the bank!"

"Oh silly me," laughed little Miss Scatterbrain.

"Of course it is. I forgot."

She smiled.

"I sometimes do, you know."

"Really?" said the bank manager.

"I'd like two, please," she said.

"Quarters?" asked the manager.

"Quarters!" agreed little Miss Scatterbrain.

The bank manager passed two shiny quarters over the counter.

Little Miss Scatterbrain looked at them.

"What are these?" she said.

"Two quarters," he replied.

"Two quarters?" she said.

"They don't look much like two chicken quarters to me!"

Eventually the bank manager managed to explain, and she gave him a fifty-cent piece, and he gave her two quarters in change. Off went little Miss Scatterbrain, to the butcher's.

"Phew!" remarked the bank manager.

Little Miss Scatterbrain walked into the butcher shop.

"Good morning," said Percy Pork, the butcher.

"Good afternoon, Mr. Beef," she replied.

"Pork!" said the butcher.

"No!" she said.

"Chicken!"

"But my name isn't Chicken!" he said.

"Of course it isn't," she replied.

"Chicken is what I'm here for!"

"Oh!" said Percy, scratching his head.

"What sort?"

"What do you suggest?" she asked.

"Roaster?" he asked.

"I thought you said your name was 'Pork'?" she said.

Percy Pork sighed a deep sigh.

"Call me Percy," he said.

Eventually, after a little more confusion, little Miss Scatterbrain managed to buy her two chicken quarters.

Percy Pork wrapped them up for her.

"Looks like snow," he said conversationally, looking out of his shop window.

"Really?" said little Miss Scatterbrain, looking at the brown paper package.

"What a funny man!" she thought to herself.

"Looks like snow indeed! Looks more like wrapped-up chicken to me!"

"Good-bye," said Percy Pork.

"Good-night," she replied, and went out to catch a bus home.

Little Miss Scatterbrain stood behind Mr. Silly in the line at the bus stop.

Along came Mr. Nosey.

He stood behind her in the line.

He looked up at the sky.

"Looks like snow!" he remarked.

Little Miss Scatterbrain looked at the brown paper package in her hand.

And said nothing!